The Spark Files

Terry Deary trained as an actor before turning to writing full time. He has many successful fiction and non-fiction children's books to his name, and is rarely out of the best-seller charts.

Barbara Allen trained and worked as a teacher and is now a full-time researcher for the Open University.

The Spark Files

Book Eight

Magical Magnets

Illustrated by Philip Reeve

faber and faber

First published in 1999
by Faber and Faber Limited
3 Queen Square, London WC1N 3AU

Printed in Italy

Cover design: Shireen Nathoo

Terry Deary and Barbara Allen are hereby identified as authors
of this work in accordance with Section 77 of the Copyright,
Designs and Patent Act 1988

A CIP record for this book
is available from the British Library

ISBN 0-571-19743-4

To Sam Goakes TD

Magical Magnets

FILE 1

NAME: Sam Spark
(That's me!)

DESCRIPTION: I may be small - but so was King Kong and he could have ruled the world. Of course I don't look like a big monkey, but I'm just as clever.

NOTES: Listen here, my name is Sam
Sammy Spark, that's who I am
If you get into a Jam
I'll save you just like Superman.

NAME: Auntie Gladys
(my Dad's oldest
sister)

DESCRIPTION: Auntie Gladys is a lot
older than Dad and behaves
like my Gran. I wish she
wouldn't spit on her hanky
and wash my face with
it. Very embarrassing.

NOTES: If you have a sweet Aunt Glad

Then you're very lucky, mate!

Ours is odd, you could say 'mad'

Glad is past her sell-by date!

FILE 3

NAME: Sally Spark
(That's me!)→

DESCRIPTION: A prisoner in Miss Cruella de Crunch's orphanage - but she can't tame me. I am ruthless, fearless and very, very clever. With my trusty four-legged friend, Boozle the dog, we stop at nothing... though Boozle can be slowed by a big, juicy bone.

NOTES: Sally Spark, an orphan child
Parents vanished in the night
I will fight and get my freedom
'Cos I am so very bright.

FILE 4

NAME: Mr Grouse

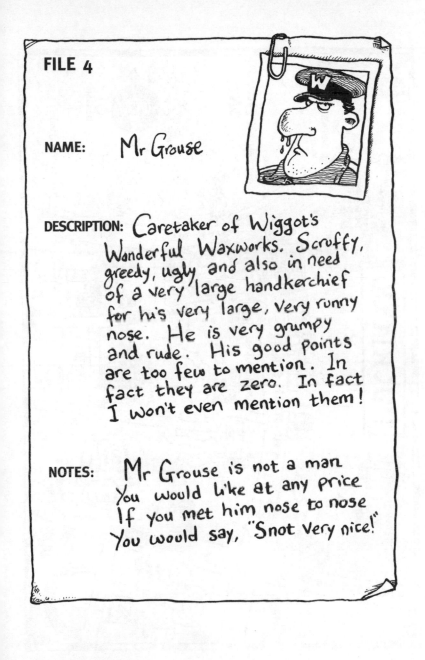

DESCRIPTION: Caretaker of Wiggot's Wonderful Waxworks. Scruffy, greedy, ugly and also in need of a very large handkerchief for his very large, very runny nose. He is very grumpy and rude. His good points are too few to mention. In fact they are zero. In fact I won't even mention them!

NOTES: Mr Grouse is not a man
You would like at any price
If you met him nose to nose
You would say, "Snot very nice!"

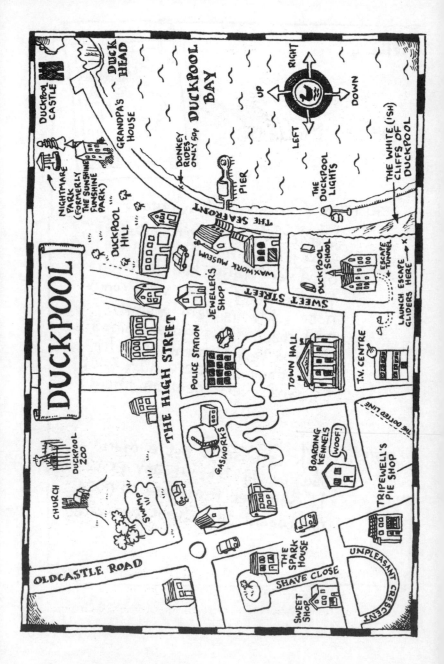

Chapter 1 – Sally's story

The wind blew wild down Duckpool High Street. It tore a tattered poster off a crumbling wall. The sign beside a shabby door said...

It was a metal noticeboard, and the paper poster was held in place by a magnet at each corner. I shuddered as I remembered my lessons on magnetism at the orphanage, where we were taught by Miss Cruella de Crunch herself...

How I hated Miss Cruella de Crunch and her science lessons. Now that I'd escaped from the clutches of Crunch I'd never go back. I put the corner of the poster back and held it down with the magnet. Then I crouched in the shelter of the doorway.

"Hush, Boozle," I said to the shaggy dog that panted by my side. "He'll be coming soon to get us!" I shivered as I looked back down the empty High Street. "Let's hide in here."

"Geruff!" Boozle agreed.

I pushed at the dark green door to Wiggot's Waxworks and slipped inside the entrance hall. A sign pointed to a gloomy stairway on the left. It said...

"I think perhaps we shouldn't go in there, Boozle." Another sign pointed down the other way. It said...

"Grrrr?" the dog asked, tilting its large head.

"I think that maybe if..." I began to say.

But suddenly Boozle's sharp ears pricked up at some small sound. Clack-click, Clack-click, Clack-click, Clack-click. Footsteps limping down the street.

"Quick, Boozle!" I cried and dragged the heavy dog along the passage to the right. It was very dark but I wasn't scared. It had been darker in Miss de Crunch's cupboard. I remembered my friends had brought me their homework in that cupboard and it saved me. It was an experiment on magnetic 'domains'. I remembered the book *Science for Dunces*...

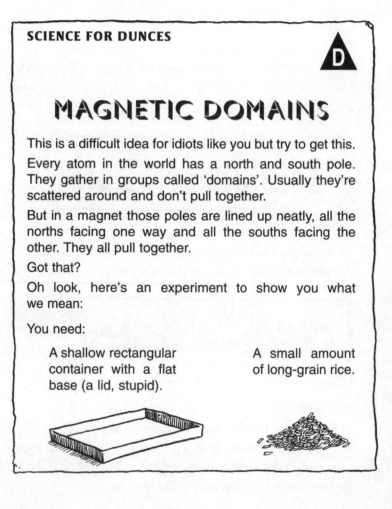

SCIENCE FOR DUNCES

MAGNETIC DOMAINS

This is a difficult idea for idiots like you but try to get this.

Every atom in the world has a north and south pole. They gather in groups called 'domains'. Usually they're scattered around and don't pull together.

But in a magnet those poles are lined up neatly, all the norths facing one way and all the souths facing the other. They all pull together.

Got that?

Oh look, here's an experiment to show you what we mean:

You need:

A shallow rectangular container with a flat base (a lid, stupid).

A small amount of long-grain rice.

What you do:

1. Put enough rice in to cover the bottom.

2. Gently tap the side of the container with your hand.

TAP TAP

3. You will find that small groups of rice begin to line up facing the same way. They are making small 'domains'.

4. In a magnet those domains all go the same way. Clever eh? Unlike you.

The orphans all brought me their rice domain home-work. I soaked the rice in the water and ate it. It isn't every day you can survive by eating your homework. I smiled when I remembered my kind orphanage friends.

Suddenly the front door to Wiggot's Waxworks flew open and hit the wall with a crash. I watched from the shadows as a man dressed in a raincoat rushed into the empty hallway. "Hello, hello, hello!" he called and waited for an answer. His hair was greasy grey and it lay flat on his skull.

A door creaked at the end of the stairway on the left and heavy boots clumped down the bare wooden stairs. An old man peered out from the foot of the staircase. He wore a navy blue uniform. His nose ran like a tap. "*Sniff!* And what do you want, mister? *Sniff!*" he asked and wiped his nose across his sleeve.

"I am a detective, and Frank Plank is my name. I guess you must be the famous Mr Wiggot, owner of this wax museum?"

"Well, you guess wrong," the old man sniffed. "My name is Grouse and I'm the famous *Sniff!* caretaker."

"Ah, Mr House, I'm looking for a girl."

"Grouse!" the old man snuffled.

"No, not a grouse, a young girl, Mr Louse."

"I meant my name is Grouse, not House or Louse," the old man shouted, "if you don't mind, Mr Crank."

"It's Plank," the grey-haired detective replied. "Frank Plank is my name – catching kids is my game."

"What sort of game is that, then, Mr Tank?"

"I catch them and send them back... because I get well paid, I can tell you, Mr Mouse. And now I'm looking for young Sally Spark. A brown-haired girl. I don't suppose you've seen her?"

And in the entrance to the Childhood Grotto I shuddered in the gloom as I heard old Plank's voice grating. He sat tiredly on a chair. "I've chased them all this rotten day," he groaned. "Her and her big dog. Caught them once," he sighed. "Bit me and got clean away."

Mr Grouse looked scared. "She's on the loose with some big biting dog?"

"Oh, no! The dog's not so bad. It's Sally Spark that bit me!" Plank replied and showed a grubby, bandaged hand. "Still, you can't miss them. Looks very much like a big, shaggy wolf."

"The girl looks like a big, shaggy wolf?" the old man gasped.

"No, no! The dog! The girl's a skinny thing with pale green eyes and dusty brown coloured hair."

"Who wants her back?" the man from Wiggot's asked.

"Her cruel and wicked orphan-keeper, of course. The same old story. Won't pay to feed the dog and wants to have it put away."

"Poor kid," the old man sighed and wiped his nose upon his jacket sleeve. "Have you no pity for this child? *Sniff!* Alone and lonely in this cruel and heartless world?" he sniffled.

"A thousand pounds reward," Frank Plank said plainly.

The old man dried his eyes. "You should have said! A thousand *Sniff!* pounds! I'll call you if I see her or her dog."

"That's right... a German Shepherd cross, by the way," Frank Plank explained.

"A German Shepherd," old Grouse gasped. "She's run off with a German Shepherd? Has he got his German sheep with him? And do the sheep bite too, then, Mr Clank?"

But Plank had gone into the grey and gusty afternoon. I slid further into the room.

"I'll take you into town for a birthday treat," my Auntie Gladys promised. "I'll buy you a nice present." Auntie Gladys was short and stout and very loud. Sometimes she could show you up. (Come to think of it all my relatives show me up.) But it was worth being shown up to get a present, I decided.

Anyway, we missed our bus stop because she was chatting to the driver. We ended up getting off the bus at the wrong end of Duckpool High Street – the grotty end where half the shops were closed and boarded up.

There was one shop still open, a second-hand book shop with piles of tatty books on a table outside being blown in the chilly wind. One flapped open and the colourful pictures caught my eye. "Stop a moment, Auntie!" I cried. I picked up the book. "Look at this! *The Young Magician's Handbook*!"

"Lots of germs in them old books," Auntie warned me.

"No! Look, this one's never been used. It still has some of the materials for the tricks in little plastic pockets!"

There were playing cards and balloons and dice and rubber spiders and magnets and pencils and even a magic wand. Auntie picked it up. "Reduced from £10 to £1! I'll buy it for your birthday," she offered.

"Thanks, Auntie," I cried. She stepped into the dusty, cobwebbed shop and came out with the book in a brown paper bag. I walked down the street with my head bent down and my eyes glued to the pages. I was so interested I almost collided with a limping man.

As we walked past some shabby green doors this limping, flat-headed man barged out muttering, "Old nutter!"

"Here, Auntie Gladys! That flat-headed feller called you an old nutter!"

"He never did!" she cried.

"I heard him with my own two eyes," I said firmly.

"The cheek," she squeaked. "How dare he call me old. I'm only twenty-two," she lied.

Then I stopped beside the green doors. "Here, Auntie Gladys," I asked. "What's a waxwork, eh?"

"It's a model made of wax, as large as life and fit to frighten the freckles off your face," my Auntie Gladys replied.

"Can I have one then, Auntie Gladys? For my birthday?"

Auntie shifted the shopping bag on her arm. "Oh no, my dear. If you want to see a stiff and ugly figure in the house, then come round to ours and take a look at your Uncle Ernie watching soccer on the telly."

"Well, can we go and see these Wiggot's Waxworks?" I whinged.

Auntie Gladys sighed and smiled. "This old place used to be the Duckpool Cinema. Your Uncle Ernie would bring me here when we were younger."

"Yeah! Trust the mean old goat to bring you to a tatty dump like this," I muttered.

"It wasn't tatty in the old days," Auntie Gladys replied. "It was called the Picture Palace and it was a palace to me."

"And I suppose Uncle Ernie was young Prince Charming," I laughed.

"It's true. And I was Cinderella," my aunt burbled happily.

"And now you're both more like the ugly sisters," I had to mumble.

"Let's go inside," my aunt said. "Let's see if it's all changed."

Auntie Gladys tugged at the creaking door and stepped into the dingy hallway. A musty smell, like damp and rotten cabbage, made my nose curl back. "Ohhhh! Yeuch!" I cried. "Smells just like our class's hamster cage."

PHEW!

But I jumped when a voice from some dark shadow grunted, "If you don't like it why not go away, *Sniff!*?"

I turned towards a small office with a glass window and a cash till. An old man squinted over the top of the till. His badge said, 'Mr Grouse'. He had a bowl of Crispy Puff cereal that was piled high in a bowl. "We've come to see the waxworks, mister," I said boldly.

Mr Grouse came out and wiped the nose-drip on his sleeve. "In that case, I'll collect your money. *Sniff!* Three pounds adults, two pounds kids. Five quid, please."

"Five pounds, you say?" gasped Auntie Gladys.

"Or ten pounds if you want to argue about it," he growled. Auntie Gladys pulled a ten pound note out of her purse. A crisp new note.

"You can have the ten pound note... if you can catch it!" I offered.

"You what?" the man blinked.

"You what?" Auntie Gladys gasped.

I smiled and looked at the *Young Magician's Handbook*. It showed me how to do the trick...

Young Magician's Handbook

The Ten Pound Twist

You need:

 A ten pound note (or a piece of paper if you can't afford the money).

You also need a volunteer – preferably someone who's not too bright.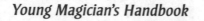

PREPARE:

Hold the note flat and let it float to the floor.

1. Offer to give the note to anyone who can catch it.

2. Fold the note in half length-wise.

OW!

3. Ask the volunteer to hold their finger and thumb a little way apart.

4. Hold the folded note between their finger and thumb, about half-way down the note.

5. Let it go.

WHAT HAPPENS: The volunteer misses the note every time. You win!

By the way... it helps if you chat to the volunteer and let the note go while you're in the middle of a sentence! That's not really cheating!

I followed the instruc-
tions. "How long have you
worked here, Mr Grouse?" I
asked. "Twenty years? That's
quite amazing! To think that
someone..." I let go of the
note. He snatched at it but
missed it.

"*Sniff!* Eh?" he cried.

"We get in free," I said happily.

"How did you do that?" Auntie Gladys asked.

"*Sniff!* Magic," Grouse grumbled.

"Science, really," I shrugged. "The most powerful
magnet in the world is the Earth itself!" I explained.

"Gawd, 'e sounds just like one of them there *Sniff!*
television programmes," Grouse muttered.

I ignored him and went on. "At the centre of the
Earth is a magnetic core – a ball of iron and nickel
2,500 km across. It pulls any material towards it at the
same speed no matter what it weighs. It takes the note less
than 0.2 seconds to fall between the fingers. It takes
0.3 seconds for Mr Grouse's brain to send a message to
his fingers to grab it. We win!" I grinned and handed the
note to Auntie Gladys.

She shrugged. "These Spark kids are clever with their
science," she said proudly.

"Spark? Did you say Spark?" Grouse asked.

"Now, where have I just heard that name?" he asked
and wiped his nose on his sleeve.

A newspaper was folded on his desk and I glanced at
the front page...

Duckpool Daily

Still only 6 pence

SCIENCE GIRL ON THE RUN

The orphan daughter of two famous scientists has gone missing from the de Crunch Home for Rich Orphans. Sally Spark (pictured, right) disappeared last night. Miss Cruella de Crunch said tearfully, "We all miss dear little Sally so much. I would give anything to get my hands on that child! In fact I'll give £1,000!"

Sally Spark was orphaned when her famous scientist parents set off to investigate strange flashing red, green and orange lights over Duckpool Hill. Earlier reports that they were a misplaced set of Duckpool Council traffic lights proved mistaken when they disappeared in the direction of Pluto. The light and the brilliant Sparks were never seen again. It is certain that they were kidnapped by aliens. The Sparks provided for poor little Sally in their will and there is an allowance of £1,000 per month for anyone caring for Sally.

Miss de Crunch said, "It's not the money – though I did point out to her that a measly £1,000 a month doesn't pay for her dog's food and the smelly creature could starve for all I care.

No, it's not the money. I love that dear little, sweet little, girl – and when I get my hands on her scrawny little neck she'll never escape again... ever! For her own good, of course."

Police Chief Constable Brick said last night, "We fear she may have been abducted by aliens and we have extra men watching every set of traffic lights in Duckpool."

"That's where I've heard the name!" the old man cried. "Is she any relation?"

"Aye!" Auntie Gladys said grimly. "She's the daughter of my youngest brother Septimus Spark, poor lad."

"My cousin," I explained. "I hope they find her."

"Nah!" Mr Grouse leered. "I hope I find her – I could use a thousand *Sniff!* quid!"

"You wouldn't betray a helpless little girl, Mr Grouse, would you?"

"Want to *Sniff!* bet?" the man hissed.

I heard the caretaker with the runny nose pick up the newspaper and I turned and ran. That's how it came about that I didn't know it was my long-lost relatives – Aunt Gladys and cousin Sam – at the front desk.

I slipped into the gloom of the Childhood Grotto and dragged Boozle after me.

The whole room looked like a forest that was filled with frozen people. But they were the sort of people that you'd only see in your most crazy dreams or in the nursery rhymes and fairy tales you hear as a toddler. Their costumes were a rainbow of colours (except for a witch who was all in black). And they were every shape and size you could imagine.

Ugly gnomes grinned at us from underneath some great green toadstools. And, at the far end of the room, a giant loomed up through the gloom. It looked as if his head could brush the roof of fairy-light stars. He'd have scared me if I hadn't had Boozle for company. My brave dog bared his teeth and a growl rumbled in his throat.

"Hush! We don't want anyone to hear us!"

A thousand little bulbs were scattered round the purple-painted ceiling. They looked just like a starry sky and gave the only light inside the mysterious room. The ceiling was a dome and I couldn't see any walls. I really could have been inside a magic forest.

Hansel and Gretel stood inside a sugar-coated cottage and pushed an old lady into a ruby-red, glowing oven. A sign by the waxworks said...

Humpty Dumpty tumbled off a wall of bright red bricks and the poem beside him read...

Humpty Dumpty sat on a wall

Humpty Dumpty had a great fall

All the King's horses and all the King's men

Had scrambled egg for breakfast

Snow White sat up smiling in her casket made of crystal while Miss Muffet screamed a frozen scream at a hairy spider coloured green and blue.

I wandered deeper into the room. Every nursery rhyme or story that I'd ever heard had a life-sized model here.

"They look so real! Almost alive!" I whispered to puzzled Boozle and stared into the great glass eyes of Goldilocks. Boozle licked his chops when he saw the plates of porridge on the table. He hadn't eaten since we left Cruella de Crunch's prison last night.

"All made of wax," I said. "You'd get more life from a penny candle."

Boozle's eyes were wider than those of a child in a toyshop and his hungry little guts rumbled as he watched old Mother Hubbard go to her bone cupboard and found it empty. I was glad he couldn't read the poem beside the waxwork!

OLD MOTHER HUBBARD
WENT TO THE CUPBOARD
TO GET HER POOR DOGGIE
A PLUM
WHEN SHE GOT THERE
THE CUPBOARD WAS BARE
SO THE DOG TOOK A BIT
OF HER BUM!

Boozle stopped and blinked at every nursery scene.

"Ahhhh! Look at those two babes in that dark wood," I told him, "Ooooh! I used to love that story there... that's where the princess kisses her prince–frog."

But Boozle had his mind set on finding food. He sniffed at every model once then hurried on again. He was out of sight for a minute and suddenly scuttled back to me, tail between his legs. "What's wrong, boy?" I asked.

He whimpered softly and stayed close to my legs as I followed the path round to Red Riding Hood's granny's cottage. We stood in the garden with its bright paper flowers and butterflies of a dozen different colours, hovering under the porch. Through the open door I could see the red-mouthed wolf in a mob cap drooling wax droplets at the thought of eating the wax Red Riding Hood. "It's not a real wolf, you daft dog!" I laughed.

There was a sudden movement in the garden and I saw what had really scared Boozle. The butterflies began moving.

For a moment I almost screamed aloud, then I sighed. "They're not real, Boozle," I muttered. "They're just using the magic of magnets." I made him sit and I said, "Remember that science magazine Mum and Dad used to buy me? There was an experiment in there..."

THE BUTTER-FLIER

Hi there, Cool Kids! Amaze your friends and impress them with your cleverness. After all, you have to be clever to be a Cool Kids magazine reader, haven't you?

YOU NEED:

A jam jar   Thread   Sticky tape   A paper clip   A magnet

TO MAKE:

1. Make a card butterfly about 2cm across. Colour it and tape a paper clip to the top and a length of thread to the bottom.

2. Tape the other end of the thread to the bottom of the jam jar so it is slightly shorter than the jar.

3. Tape a magnet to the inside of the lid and put the lid on the jar.

4. Gather your friends around – and you'll have lots of friends if you do wonderful tricks like this… except the jealous ones who will probably try to beat you to a pulp. Say, "I am going to make this butterfly fly!" "Oooh!" your friends will cry. Tip the jar upside down so the butterfly is hanging by the thread. "Ohhh!" Your friends will cry. "It's not really flying! It's hanging by the thread!"

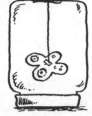

5. Then you turn the jar the right way up and watch the gasp as the butterfly stays up in the air! Little do they know it's the magnetic force of the magnet on the paper clip that is keeping it there!

I whispered, "There's probably a magnet in the porch roof and the butterflies all have little metal strips on top!"

But Boozle still wasn't happy.

"Yes, Boozle, I know what you're thinking. How come the butterflies are moving about like that?"

"Ruff!" he growled.

"Well, it's probably a slight draught!"

"Ruff?"

"Where's the draught coming from? Probably someone opened the door to the Childhood Grotto and they're… ohhhh!"

I felt a shiver run down my spine and it didn't stop till it reached my big toes. "I see what you mean, Boozle! Someone's come in! Probably that snotty caretaker, the tubby woman and the scruffy boy! They'll find us and take us back to Miss de Crunch's. She'll lock me away and starve you to death! We're trapped, Boozle! And there's no place to hide!"

Chapter 4 – Sam's story

Mr Grouse was grumpy because of the way we'd outwitted him over the entrance money. "Do you have a guide book?" Auntie Gladys asked.

"Follow your nose, *Sniff!*" the man muttered and turned back to his bowl of Crispy Puff cereal.

"You must have trouble following your nose, Mr Grouse," I said.

"*Sniff!* Why's that?" he asked.

"Because it never stops running," I told him.

His thin mouth curled down at the corners. He leaned forward and said, "You'd better keep out of our Nightmare Castle room," he said quietly.

"Why? Is it too scary?" I asked.

"No! It's just a waste of money for someone like you. It's full of ugly monsters and beasties, and you can see something that ugly any time – in a mirror!"

"Monsters and beasties!" Auntie Gladys said with a shudder. "Enough to give you nightmares. It wasn't like this when my Ernie brought me here." She looked around at peeling paint held onto crumbling walls by spiders' webs.

The old man stuck a dripping nose an inch or two from hers. "If you don't like it I can tell you what to do..."

Auntie Gladys fixed him with her best stare – the one that turns cats to stone. She snapped her fingers at me. "Sam? Do you have that balloon from the *Young Magician's Handbook*?"

I didn't know why she wanted it but I knew it would be something nasty. I passed it to her and Mr Grouse and I watched her without a word. "Here's a little magic I learned when I used to help your Uncle Ernie on stage."

Auntie Gladys blew up the balloon, rubbed it on her sweater and suddenly held it over the caretaker's bowl of Crispy Puff cereal. The cereal leapt out of the bowl.

"Hey! That's me tea!" the man cried.

Auntie Gladys ignored his protests. "Everything is made up of atoms, Sam."

"I know Auntie."

"And atoms are made up of equal numbers of protons and electrons. Rubbing the balloon picks up electrons from the wool. Those electrons are desperate to find some protons to team up with, so they make a grab for the protons in the Crispy Puffs! See?"

"Like a magnet! Magic!" I grinned.

"No, not magic. Science! All us Spark family have always been good at science. Of course science looks like magic to simple-minded people," she said, giving the caretaker a hard look. "That's how your Uncle Ernie and I made a living for years."

"Why did you give up?" Grouse asked.

Auntie Gladys clutched at her throat. "It's a sad and tragic tale, Mr Grouse, one that would bring tears to a potato's eyes!"

"Tell me?"

Auntie dabbed at her eyes with a few crumbs of Crispy Puff cereal from the balloon.

"It all went tragically wrong one night at Wigan Empire Theatre. Ernie had a marvellous new trick. You know magicians who saw a lady in half, Mr Grouse?"

"*Sniff!* Yeah?"

"My Ernie decided to saw himself in half!"

"What happened?"

"Well, he sawed his legs off, didn't he? He got the angles all wrong! You should have seen the expression on his face when his legs fell onto the stage and rolled into the stalls! It took them a week to mop up the blood!"

"But how come he's not dead?" I whispered. "And he was walking around the garden when we left the house!"

Auntie Gladys ignored me. "He died instantly," she sighed. "His legs lived a little longer. They say they can still be seen kicking around Wigan Empire Theatre."

Mr Grouse turned pale. "That's put me right off me *Sniff!* tea!" he wailed.

Auntie Gladys looked under the lapel of her coat and pulled out a pin. She stuck it in the balloon. The balloon popped and the Crispy Puff cereal flew all over Mr Grouse's desk.

Auntie Gladys held the pin under his nose as he looked at the wreckage of his snack. "That'll teach you to be more polite to visitors, my man! Now, what is along that corridor?"

Mr Grouse wiped his nose on his sleeve. "*Sniff!* We have the Childhood Grotto in there," he muttered sulkily.

"Sounds grotty," I said.

"Then why don't you try this door over here?" old Grouse asked with a wiggle of his thumb.

"Oh? And where does that lead?" I asked.

"It leads back to the street!" the caretaker cackled. "If you don't want to see the show then go away. Doesn't bother me 'cos I don't own the place. Anyway, we close at half-past five!" he warned us.

"What time is it now?" I asked.

He snapped on a small radio that stood on a shelf behind his desk...

... THE TIME IS JUST COMING UP TO FIVE O'CLOCK. AND HERE IS THE SIX O'CLOCK NEWS. POLICE ARE STILL HUNTING THE MISSING DUCKPOOL GIRL, SALLY SPARK. SHE HAS BEEN SEEN TO THE NORTH OF DUCKPOOL ON A BUS, TO THE SOUTH OF DUCKPOOL ON THE BACK OF A TANDEM, TO THE WEST OF DUCKPOOL ON A PONY AND TO THE EAST OF DUCKPOOL ON A BOUNCY CASTLE. POLICE CHIEF CONSTABLE BRICK SAID, "WE ARE TAKING SERIOUSLY ALL SALLY SPARK SIGHTINGS, EVEN THE SILLY-AS-A-SAUSAGE SIGHTINGS. WE WILL LEAVE NO TURN UN-STONED TILL SHE IS SAFE."

POLICE ARE WATCHING ALL TRAFFIC LIGHTS AND STOPPING SUSPICIOUS BUSES, TANDEMS, HORSES AND BOUNCY CASTLES...

"*Sniff!* Poor kid," Mr Grouse sighed.

Auntie Gladys pulled a tissue from her handbag. "I suggest you use that, Mr Grouse," she said sweetly.

"To mop up me Crispy Puff cereal?"

"No! To mop up your nose." She turned to me. "Now let's have a look inside this Childhood Grotto shall we, Sam?"

I led the way down the gloomy corridor where the loudest noise was the spiders tramping over their webs, and I threw open the doors.

"Ooooh!" I gasped.

"Aaaah!" Auntie Gladys sighed.

And we walked into something that looked like a magic wood.

Chapter 5 – Sam's story

I set off along the forest trail and soon left Auntie Gladys far behind.

The place was creepy with these greasy-faced figures standing there like corpses in a graveyard. Their glassy eyes followed you as you walked. Even the stupid-looking giant that loomed over the trees was about as lively as Class 4 in one of Miss Trout's history lessons.

Of course I wasn't scared myself, but I'd have thought that little kids would be wetting their nappies at some of the fairy-tale creatures.

Especially when one of them moved!

I was just passing a kitchen where Cinderella was on her knees, scrubbing the floor, when I saw her out of the corner of my eye. Her scrubbing brush moved forward. "Wahhhh!" I gasped. I wasn't scared! I really wasn't! But I dropped my birthday-present book on the floor and bent to pick it up.

I wasn't really looking at the book. My eyes were fixed on the moving brush. Backwards and forwards it went, yet the face was wax and the eyes were glass. How did Wiggot's waxworks move, I wondered?

I looked down at my book and it had fallen open. I stared at it for a moment and then grinned. Of course! That was it!

The Magical Magnet Theatre

You need:

A large shoebox with a lid, two sticks around 30cm (or two 30cm rulers), white card, sticky tape, scissors, paper clips, glue, colouring materials.

To make:

1. Glue the shoebox onto its lid. Make a cut-out in each end of the lid.

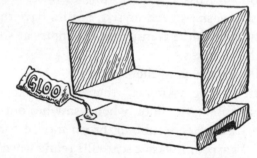

2.

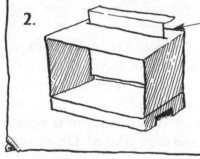

Cut a slot in the top of the box and make a card backdrop to fit into it. Make as many as you like – one for each scene.

3. Draw your characters on card and fold the bottom to make a base. Tape a paper clip to the base of each character.

4. Fasten a magnet to one end of each stick. Put the characters on stage. Slide the magnets through the cut-out and under the stage. Use the sticks to move the characters.

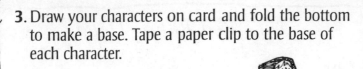

Fold ⟶

Amazing! How does it work? Because a magnet's power can travel through a non-magnetic material. That's a very useful thing to know.

I turned the page and there was even a script to get a Magical Magnet Theatre performance going. The trouble is it was such a dreadful script you wouldn't want to see it! You do? Oh, very well. But you've been warned...

Little Red Riding Hood

Cast:

Little Red Riding Hood

Mrs Hood
(her Mum)

Granny Hood
(her Gran)

Robin Hood
(her Dad)

Baron Hardup
(her evil Landlord)

Mr Wolf
(a wolf)

Scene 1 – Little Red Riding Hood's cottage. Mrs Hood at the door. Baron Hardup knocks. (Sound-effect – knock on something wooden like your Dad's head.)

Baron: Well, Mrs Hood, I've come for my rent!

Mrs Hood: A tent? You want to borrow a tent?

Baron: Where is my rent?

Mrs Hood: Went!

Baron: Rent's went?

Mrs Hood: Spent!

Baron: You went and spent the rent?

Mrs Hood: In Kent.

Baron: You went and spent the rent in Kent?

Mrs Hood: I never meant!

Baron: Give me five pounds at once or out of my cottage you go!

Mrs Hood: Here's a fiver.

Baron: (*Examines it. To Little Red Riding Hood*) Counterfeit!

Little Red Riding Hood: She has two!

Baron: Counterfeit! Not count-her-feet! Worthless money! I want real money or else.

Mrs Hood: Nothing else for it, Little Red Riding Hood. You'll have to scrounge a fiver off your Gran. Off you go through the dark and evil wood. Don't stop to talk to no wicked wolves, mind!

End of scene 1.

You can write the rest yourself. You can't do any worse!

I closed my book and turned back onto the path. I peered along a tunnel made in the trees and noticed a signpost hanging neatly on a bush.

TO RED RIDING HOOD'S
GRANNY'S COTTAGE

Amazing! Just the story I'd been reading! It was an omen! I set off to explore.

Twigs and leaves and roots were in a tangle on the floor. I really felt that I was walking in a magic wood. The twisting path led to a cottage in a little clearing. The door was open so, of course, I had to look inside.

Red Riding Hood stood silently beside an old brass bed, a basket full of fruit upon her arm. And, in the bed, there lay the Wolf. Old, ugly, with silver eyes, yellow fangs and a bright red tongue. It looked quite funny in that lace-trimmed cap and Granny's flannel nightie.

I wiped a finger over Granny's fruit. "Huh. Wax!" I snorted. I was hungry and an apple would have come in handy. "And dusty," I added, looking at my blackened finger. Then I saw the sign...

PLEASE DO NOT
TOUCH THE MODELS

So, of course, I had to.

I'm the kind of boy who always has to do the things he was told not to. I wandered over to the bed.

"Hiya, Wolfy-Wolfy-Wolfy! Who's afraid of the big bad Wolf then?" I tipped the lace cap over one grey and wolfish ear. Then I slipped the glasses down the whiskery nose.

The Granny–Wolf looked drunk. I giggled and laughed until it hurt. "My-oh-my, Granny, what big teeth you've got!" I cried and put my hand into the model's mouth to pull the shiny tongue.

That was when the Wolf's jaws shut with a mighty snap.

I pulled my hand out as the jaws closed but the teeth still nipped my finger ends.

I just stared at first. The Wolf seemed stiff and quiet as ever.

"Was it a dream?" I wondered. Then my finger ends began to hurt.

I turned and ran. I ran back through the trees, stumbling over tangled roots and twigs.

"Oh, Auntie Gladys!" I cried. "Oh, Auntie Gladys! I've just been bitten by a wolf!"

Chapter 6 – Sally's story

"Oh, Boozle!" I moaned. "He'll run and tell that nasty Plank."

The dog shook off the cap and glasses then he moved to rub himself against my leg. "There's no way out. We're trapped in here," I sighed. "And I was sure they'd never find us here."

"They won't if you don't want them to!" a deep voice rumbled softly from the dark sky.

I blinked and Boozle's hair bristled. "Who's there?"

"Allow me to introduce myself," the voice said.

"My name is Wiggot and I welcome you to my waxworks!"

"Where are you?" I asked.

"I can see you but you probably can't see me. Don't worry. I don't mean you any harm. I often get strange people escaping in here."

"Escaping from what?"

"From the nasty world outside. I always try to help them!" The voice sounded kind enough. "So what's your story, young lady?"

"I'm Sally Spark... and this is my dog, Boozle... say hello, Boozle!"

"Ruff?" the dog growled, tilting its head to one side and looking stupidly towards the purple sky.

"Hello, Boozle," the voice replied. The cowardly mutt tried to hide under the bed but that was where I'd hidden the waxworks of Red Riding Hood and the Wolf.

"I'm on the run from Cruella de Crunch's orphanage," I explained.

"You can stay here," Mr Wiggot's voice said. "I need a little help to move the magnetic waxworks and really spook the visitors."

"Which are they?" I asked.

There was a long silence. "You know... I'm sure I can't remember. Sorry, Sally, sounds silly... but I can't remember where they all are. They could be lost for ever!"

"No problem, Mr Wiggot!" I cried. "There's a way to find magnets, didn't you know?"

"No."

"It was a little game Miss de Crunch had, called 'Spot the Magnet'!"

"I've played 'Spot the Traffic Warden' in the local paper... but I never win. Is it anything like that?"

"Sort of. What Miss de Crunch said was..."

50

"I gathered the orphans around and told them...

AS YOU KNOW, THE EARTH IS A HUGE MAGNET. THE NORTH POLE WILL ALWAYS ATTRACT ONE END OF A MAGNET - THE END WE CALL THE NORTH!

IF WE PLACE A COMPASS OVER THE BOX IT WILL POINT TO THE NORTH END OF THE MAGNET - BECAUSE THE MAGNET IN THE BOX IS NEARER THAN THE NORTH POLE.

WE NEED TWO PLASTIC BOWLS (A LARGE AND A SMALL) STICKY TAPE, A BAR MAGNET, A PEN, WATER.

Magnet
large bowl
Pen
small bowl
Tape
Water

FIRST MAKE A FREE-FLOATING MAGNET: TAPE THE BAR MAGNET IN THE SMALL PLASTIC BOWL. FLOAT THE SMALL BOWL IN THE LARGER BOWL WITH WATER IN. THE NORTH END OF THE MAGNET WILL FACE THE NORTH POLE!

Small bowl   Magnet
Large bowl   Water

"The compass worked," I told the voice of Mr Wiggot. "We found the hidden magnet and we all put a cross in the same place. We all won our supper that night. Miss de Crunch was furious and she guessed that I was the one who solved the problem."

"Never mind, Sally, you're safe here," the voice said.

There was a lot of shouting going on in the corridor outside the Childhood Grotto and I knew they'd be coming back.

"I don't think I am safe, Mr Wiggot," I said. "Poor Boozle went and nipped that boy... he ran to tell the snotty caretaker. They'll call for Plank – and then we're caught!"

"Don't worry," the voice said. "There's a way to keep you safe... show me where you hid the waxwork wolf and then we'll do what must be done..."

Chapter 7 – Sam's story

Back in the office Auntie Gladys was fussing over my bleeding hand. "You should have told us that the waxworks moved," she sobbed and tears splashed on the dusty floor.

"The waxworks move? Oh, give me *Sniff!* strength!" the old man scoffed and flicked his fingers through the phone book. "Here we are... Frank Plank, Detective and Kid-catcher, Duckpool 5432."

"If Sam says the waxwork moved, the waxwork moved – he never lies – and what are these wolf teeth-marks doing in his hand?" she snapped.

"Not wolf... just dog. There's some wild dog that's on the loose and some mad, biting girl," the caretaker explained and dialled 5-4-3-2. "Is that Hank Prank?"

he asked. "About that thousand pounds reward... I've found your wolf and Sally Spark... come to Wiggot's right away!"

"A thousand pounds!" I gasped. "A thousand pounds. I reckon half of that belongs to me."

"At least!" Auntie Gladys agreed. "At least! Maybe even two halves... you risked your precious hand," she said, and patted my head.

"Some chance," Grouse muttered and he hurried out to meet the great detective.

"I'll sort that wolf out, Auntie Gladys," I said.

"Ooooh! You don't want to go back in there unless you have a big stick!" she breathed.

"You're right," I said. "So you know about the magnets, do you?"

"What do you mean?" she asked.

"I mean, that wolf is worked by magnets, I reckon. I'm going back in there to take the magnetism out of the magnets! He'll never bite a boy or maul a man or worry a woman or grab a girl ever again!"

"But how can you take magnetism out of magnets?" Auntie Gladys asked. "Not even your Uncle Ernie could do that and he was a magician... until he swallowed a sword and cut his throat."

I blinked. "I thought you said he sawed himself in half."

Auntie Gladys blushed. "He sawed himself in half after he cut his throat."

I did think she might be lying. But I pulled the Basho comic from my pocket and showed her how it worked...

2 USE THE NAIL TO PICK UP AS MANY PAPER CLIPS AS IT WILL HOLD. SAY YOU HAVE FOUR: TELL THE KID,

MY SCORE IS FOUR. I'LL BET YOU CAN'T BEAT THAT!

3 THIS IS THE MEAN AND NASTY BIT! AS YOU PASS THE NAIL TO THE KID DROP IT ON THE TABLE OR THE FLOOR.

(IF IT DOESN'T HIT SOMETHING HARD, HAVE A SNEAKY HIT AT IT WITH THE HAMMER.)

4 WHEN THE KID TRIES TO PICK UP THE PAPER CLIPS THE MAGNETISM WILL BE SO WEAK THEY'LL BE LUCKY TO PICK UP ONE! TELL THEM YOU WERE BETTING THEIR WEEK'S POCKET MONEY AND TAKE IT OFF THEM!

WAH

WHAT HAPPENED? AS SOON AS YOU DROPPED THE MAGNET ALL THOSE STRAIGHT DOMAINS WERE SHAKEN UP AGAIN! IF YOU WANT TO WRECK A MAGNET, DROP IT!

BOINK!

IF YOU WANT TO LOOK AFTER A MAGNET, HANDLE IT CAREFULLY AND NEVER DROP IT. HEATING A MAGNET WILL ALSO WRECK THE DOMAINS, SO KEEP IT COOL. IF YOU HAVE A HORSESHOE MAGNET THEN PUT A PIECE OF IRON ACROSS EACH TIP. IT'S CALLED A 'KEEPER'. IT JOINS THE POLES AND KEEPS THE DOMAINS IN ORDER.

AND IF YOU WANT TO BE REALLY, REALLY NASTY TO YOUR WORST ENEMY, TAKE THEIR FAVOURITE CASSETTE TAPE AND REWIND IT BY HAND WHILE RUBBING A MAGNET OVER THE TAPE. THE SOUNDS ARE STORED IN MAGNETIC PATTERNS. RUBBING A DIFFERENT MAGNET AGAINST THE TAPE WILL WRECK THE PATTERNS! HEH! HEH! HEH!

"Mr Grouse won't like you mashing his magnets," Auntie Gladys whispered.

"Mr Grouse is outside waiting for Frank Plank. He thinks Red Riding Hood's waxwork and the wolf are Sally and her dog. But I know they're not!"

"What if they are?"

"Then they'll get a very nasty shock when I smack them!" I told her. "And we get the thousand pounds reward! Now let's get in there before Plank arrives to spoil the fun! This way, Auntie. Mind the Wolf don't get you!"

"Wolf? Get me? You never fear," she said and waved her brolly in the air. "Bite my little Sam, would he? Let me get my hands on him."

"Look! There he is, Auntie. In the cottage. See, he's underneath the quilt," I hissed.

"Three," said Auntie quite softly.

"Two," I said.

"One," Auntie said.

"Go!" I yelled.

Auntie Gladys dived on the bedspread. Bedsprings twanged and then they broke. A grey wolf-head rolled on the floor as Auntie pounced with her brolly. Wax and fur and wire and glass eyes flew across the cottage floor.

Meanwhile I had pounced and shredded poor Red Riding Hood's red cloak. I sat among the lifeless tangle of arms and legs and stuffing.

Auntie grinned. "Well, at least we've proved it's not our Sally. I don't suppose we get the thousand pounds for this?"

"A thousand pounds in bills, more like!" a giant voice boomed from somewhere in the shadows. "A thousand pounds should pay for two new models and the bed that you've just wrecked!"

We froze like frightened rabbits caught in a car's headlights. "Who said that?" Auntie squealed.

"It's Mr Wiggot!" I guessed. "He has the power to see into this room... hidden cameras, I suppose." I raised my head and called out to the spangled roof, "I'm sor-rrry, Mr Wigg-ggot! I can exxx-plain..."

"And as for you... yes, you... the fat old lady!" the voice rumbled on. "Your brolly's done more damage than a bomb. I think that you should pay for half!"

I helped Auntie to her feet but she smacked me on the knuckles with her bent brolly.

"I think I'll tell your Dad to stop your pocket money till you've paid for this," she snapped at me. "It should be paid for in fifty years or so." She marched me towards the door.

That's when the giant moved...

Chapter 8 – Sam's story

The giant moved away from the beanstalk where he'd been leaning and strode over the garden of the three little pigs towards us. I think Auntie Gladys may have been a little bit scared because her mouth was moving like a goldfish but no sound was coming out.

"You're a real live giant!" I said, and my voice came out in a squeak.

"No, I'm just a very tall man," he said and his voice was the voice of Mr Wiggot. "I own these waxworks and I keep an eye on them. I feel safe in here. Out there in the street people point at me. Nasty nippers call me names, and brutish boys throw stones. Just because I'm different!"

Auntie Gladys recovered a little, reached up and patted his hand. "It must be a lonely life, chuck."

"It was until I met a girl called Sally Spark. She's in danger on the streets too. I hoped she might move in to Red Riding Hood's granny's cottage and keep me company. I was going to try to find her family – a family called the Sparks. She thought they might be able to help her!"

"So she is in here?" I cried.

"And she's your long-lost cousin Sally!" Auntie Gladys cried.

"And it was her dog that bit me!" I complained.

"It was – but I saw it all," Mr Wiggot told me. "You pulled its tongue. You asked for it."

"Yeah," I muttered, a little ashamed.

"Time to say you are sorry," Mr Wiggot said. He looked up and called, "Sally!"

There was no reply, but the door swung open and Mr Grouse put his head in. "You called, Mr Wiggot, *Sniff!* sir?"

"I did. Have you seen a girl and a dog?" the giant asked.

"*Sniff!* Seen them! I'll say I have. I've just handed the girl over to a detective, Mr Stank! As soon as she stepped into the corridor he nabbed her. He'll deliver her back to her orphanage tomorrow morning as soon as it opens!"

Mr Wiggot groaned. "We have to get her back and set her free!"

"There's a thousand pounds reward," Mr Grouse grumbled. "He promised me!"

"And I'll give you two thousand if you get her back," the owner of the waxworks offered. He ducked through the doorway and headed for the front door. The scruffy dog lay there with its nose pressed against the door and it whimpered. "Boozle can follow her scent!" the giant cried and rubbed the dog's shaggy head.

We opened the door a crack and the wind whistled in. It was dark now. Too dark. Night had fallen but the street lights hadn't come on.

"What's happening?" Auntie Gladys asked.

Mr Grouse snapped on the radio behind his desk...

... AND WITH THE TIME AT FIVE THIRTY HERE IS THE TEN O'CLOCK NEWS. DUCKPOOL STREET LIGHTS HAVE FAILED. SHORTLY AFTER THE RED, GREEN AND ORANGE LIGHTS APPEARED OVER DUCKPOOL THE STREET LIGHTS BEGAN TO GO OUT. SCIENTISTS AT OLDCASTLE POWER STATION SAY SOMETHING MAY BE DRAINING THE POWER FROM THE STREET LIGHTING GRID. NORMAL SERVICE WILL BE RESUMED AS SOON AS POSSIBLE CRACKLE CRACKLE crackle...

"Radio's gone," Mr Grouse moaned. "Flat battery."

"We'll need a torch," I said. "It's dark out there!"

"I have one!" Mr Grouse offered. He flicked at the switch. The bulb glowed orange and then went out. "Flat battery again!" he cried.

"Then we'll have to make a battery!" Mr Wiggot said. "Mr Grouse, bring me all the copper coins from the till! Gladys, make some salty water from the staff kitchen. Sam! Bring some cooking foil from the cupboard under the sink and a pair of kitchen scissors from the drawer!"

"You can't make a battery!" I argued.

But I was wrong. Even a Spark family scientist doesn't know everything.

Mr Wiggot took an old and dusty book from the shelf. The paper was yellow with age. The cover said, *The Boy Scout's Camping Book*.

"I never knew you were a boy scout," Mr Grouse marvelled. "How on earth did you fit into them little tents?"

"They used me for a tent pole," Mr Wiggot sighed softly. He opened the book and passed it to me...

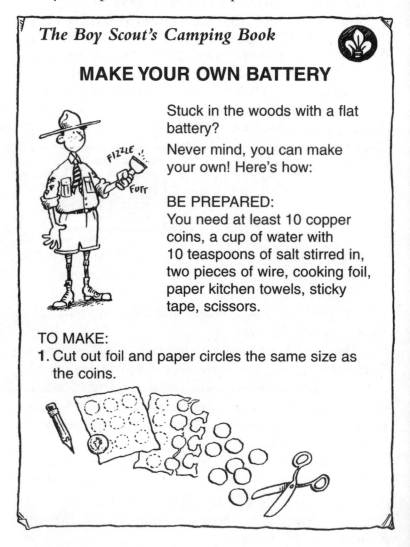

The Boy Scout's Camping Book

MAKE YOUR OWN BATTERY

Stuck in the woods with a flat battery?

Never mind, you can make your own! Here's how:

BE PREPARED:
You need at least 10 copper coins, a cup of water with 10 teaspoons of salt stirred in, two pieces of wire, cooking foil, paper kitchen towels, sticky tape, scissors.

TO MAKE:
1. Cut out foil and paper circles the same size as the coins.

2. Soak the paper discs in the salt water.

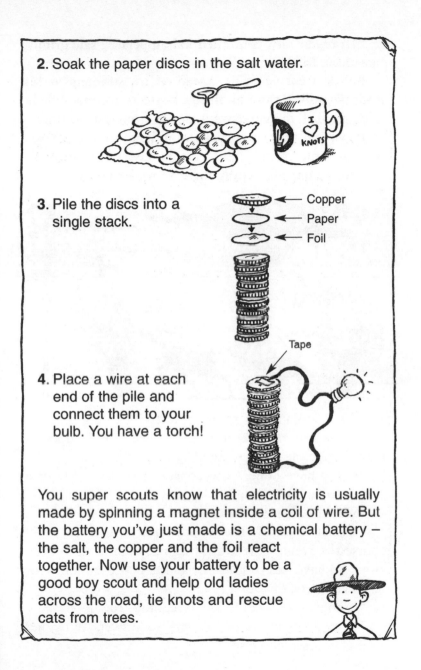

3. Pile the discs into a single stack.

Copper
Paper
Foil

Tape

4. Place a wire at each end of the pile and connect them to your bulb. You have a torch!

You super scouts know that electricity is usually made by spinning a magnet inside a coil of wire. But the battery you've just made is a chemical battery – the salt, the copper and the foil react together. Now use your battery to be a good boy scout and help old ladies across the road, tie knots and rescue cats from trees.

"Or rescue girls from their kidnappers!" I said grimly. "Lead on, Mr Wiggot!"

Boozle went snuffling ahead of us, straining at his lead. We walked through the dark streets, the moon flickering through the windswept clouds from time to time.

A young policeman was standing on the corner, watching the traffic lights. He looked up in surprise. "Good evening all... chilly night to walk the dog."

"We're looking for a young, lost girl. Pale green eyes and brownish hair. You haven't seen her, I suppose, officer?" Auntie Gladys asked.

"I may have done," the constable smiled. "About a quarter of an hour ago."

"Was she alone?" Grouse asked quickly.

"Alone! Alone?" the young officer laughed. "Of course the young lady wasn't alone. If she'd have been alone I'd have had to take her to the police station – for her own safety, of course."

"Who was with her?" Mr Wiggot asked.

The policeman craned his neck to answer. "Why, her dad, of course, who else?"

"Her dad's been kidnapped by aliens," Auntie Gladys groaned.

"Funny you should say that," the policeman said and scratched a spot between his large ears and his large helmet. "Aliens, eh? I'm on duty here keeping an eye on this one!" he said, jerking a thumb at the traffic light.

"But didn't Sally tell you who she was?" the giant asked gently.

"Ah, no, she couldn't, you see? Her dad's hand was wrapped around her mouth. She couldn't talk."

"Didn't you think that was strange?" exasperated Auntie Gladys gasped.

"I'm not completely stupid," the policeman sniffed. "I asked the gent why he was doing that..."

"And?" I urged.

"And he said she had just returned from visiting the dentist. He was afraid the chilly wind would hurt the poor child's sore gums."

"I don't believe it!" Auntie Gladys groaned.

"Oh, I believed it," the constable chuckled.

"I mean," Auntie Gladys said slowly, "I don't believe a man could be as stupid as you. Who would want to visit a dentist at this time of night?"

The policeman looked a little downcast. "Never thought of that," he admitted.

Chapter 9 – Sam's story

We must have looked an odd group as we trooped along the pavement. Boozle in front... the policeman now trailing behind, talking to himself.

"Kidnap!" he cried. "Well I never. Fancy that! I wondered why she was trying to bite her dad's hand and kicking out at him. All my months of training at the police college. And I never spotted that chap's game. They only teach us about yellow lines and helping children across the road. Caw! What a failure. The lads won't half scoff at me when I get back. They make enough fun of my name. Arthur Constable. Half-a-constable they used to call me. I reckon they could be right."

"Constable," Auntie Gladys called over her shoulder.

"Yes, ma'am?"

"Stop that whingeing."

"Yes, ma'am."

Boozle was now winding through the dark streets. His thick tail began wagging as the trail became stronger. We left the High Street far behind with its shuttered stores. We passed the car park, passed the railway station. We crossed the road at the new flats and headed towards the oldest part of town.

Dockyard Street was dark and narrow. There were dingy offices and shops and a huge scrapyard. Boozle began to trot quite quickly. Auntie Gladys panted. Old Grouse sniffled. "Use your hanky," Auntie snapped.

Then the dog stopped by a doorway. "Constable," Grouse the old caretaker croaked softly. "Bring that big torch over here."

The policeman hurried to obey him. "Yes, sir?"

"Shine it on this doorway here."

The torch connected and lit up a nameplate. It was a tarnished brass plate with small black letters. It said...

NO 13
FRANK PLANK
PRIVATE DETECTIVE
NO CASE TOO BIG –
NO FEE TOO SMALL

The policeman frowned. "You don't need to hire a private detective. We've got detectives on the police force. I fancy being a detective myself, to tell the truth."

Auntie Gladys gave a tired sigh. "You silly boy. This is the man we are looking for. He has kidnapped Sally for the reward money. Now we have to rescue her."

The dog was growling softly. Mr Wiggot reached to pat his head. "Good boy, Boozle, you led us to her. Frank Plank's office... not his home."

"Well done, Boozle!" the policeman smiled. "Now I'll arrest him."

"No," Auntie moaned. "He hasn't really broken the law. He's just returning Sally to her rightful guardian – Miss de Crunch. We don't want that. We want to care for her ourselves in the Spark Family."

"I see! I see! And what right have you to do that?" the policeman asked and drew himself up importantly.

"Oh... I'm her granny, " Auntie Gladys lied.

"Well... that's all right then... I suppose."

"And this here is her grand-dad... aren't you dear?" she went on. She nudged old Grouse firmly in the ribs with an arrow-sharp elbow.

"I am?" the old man gasped.

"You are," I put in. "And I'm her brother."

Everybody turned and looked at Mr Wiggot for support. "Ah... er... oh... I'm her great-uncle."

The constable shrugged. "You're certainly a great something." He looked at Auntie Gladys. "I see your point. It's not a police matter... but still, I'd like to help the little girl."

"And so you shall. You all shall help," Auntie said. "Gather round, now. Here's my plan..."

The only light at number 13 Dockyard Street came from a window at the back. It was a tall, black-bricked building with rusted drainpipes falling off the walls and faded paint peeling from grubby window frames.

Mr Wiggot picked me up as if I were light as a pink balloon. I perched on the giant's shoulders and looked into the office. A man was sitting at the desk. He had greasy grey hair that lay flat against his skull. His back was to the window so he didn't see me looking in.

The room was full of files and boxes. Papers spilled out onto the floor. Dirty tea mugs, phones and ashtrays, broken pens, half-eaten biscuits, packets of paper-clips and rubber bands filled the desk tops. But in the middle of the floor was a metal chair.

And on the chair was a girl. Her hands and feet were bound to the chair with sticking tape and the loose ends

were knotted. Around her mouth was another piece of tape. It was fastened cruelly tight. Her green eyes flashed with anger as she struggled with the binding.

Frank Plank finished wrapping bandage round his bleeding hand. The small window at the top was open. It let in fresh air and let the detective's words come out.

"You silly girl. You'll not get free. You'll not untie my knots. I used to be in the Brownies... or do I mean the Cubs? Anyway, they taught me to make good knots. Now, if you promise to be good – no more bites and screams – I'll take that gag from your mouth. Promise?"

But Sally Spark shook her head fiercely. Frank Plank shrugged. "Oh, please yourself... stay like that until morning. Then I'll call Miss de Crunch and claim the cash."

The detective tilted back his chair and placed his feet on the desk.

I patted Mr Wiggot on the head. That was the signal for me to be lowered. In the darkest shadows of the back yard old Grouse and Auntie waited. "Yes. She's there," I panted. "So is Frank Plank. He's fastened her to a chair."

"If I lifted you to that window could you get through and set her free?" Mr Wiggot asked.

I groaned, "That gap's just too small. It needs to be unfastened from the inside."

"You mean that you're too fat, *Sniff!*" Grouse grumbled.

"Don't be cruel and wipe your nose," Auntie Gladys said sharply. "We'll just have to use plan number two. We'll have to get the girl to the window! You can get your hands through that gap and unfasten her."

"She can't move," I argued.

"But a powerful magnet can pull her chair to the window, you can reach in, free her and she can unfasten the window."

"My magic magnets won't pull a girl on a chair!" I argued.

"No, but an electromagnet might!"

"It's in my *Young Magician's Handbook*!" I said, and turned to it.

Straw Draw

You need: A large steel nail, a battery, a drinking straw, 150cm of wire.

What you do:

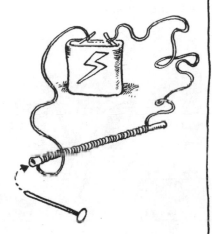

1. Connect one end of the wire to one battery terminal.

2. Wrap the wire in a coil around the straw.

3. Place the nail inside the straw.

4. Connect the other end of the wire and show the audience only the straw!

Ladies and gentlemen, I proudly present the straw that acts as a magnet!

With a roll of the drums use the straw to pick up a paper clip!

Magic!

"Our battery isn't strong enough to attract a chair! We need a huge electromagnet," I argued.

"Leave that to me, Sam," Auntie whispered. "Run round to the front and tell that daft policeman he'll have to do his part. Remember... he must knock loudly so we hear at the back and know when to start."

I scuttled off around the block as fast as my tired legs would carry me.

Chapter 10 – Sam's story

PC Constable took out his truncheon and cracked it on Frank Plank's front door. The faded paint turned to powder and was blown down Dockyard Street. I hid in the doorway of number 12 and waited breathless until the private detective came to answer.

At last the door creaked open. "Hello?" said Plank.

"Hello, hello, hello," the slow policeman said.

"What's wrong? What's wrong? What's wrong?" the flat-headed man asked.

"Ah! What indeed!" PC Constable smiled. "I saw your light... I thought you might have burglars in."

"Hah!" Plank laughed. "So, you make enough noise to wake the dead. You'd have scared any burglars off."

"That's the idea, sir."

"No it's not!" Frank fumed. "Your job is to catch the villains. I should know. I'm a detective."

"Oh? A detective? In that case you may be able to help me catch this burglar. Let me show you his picture." And PC Constable pulled a plastic wallet from his pocket, shook it and showed it to Frank Plank. To be honest the policeman didn't have a picture but I'd remembered something I'd seen on television the week before...

HI KIDS! DO YOU WANT A LITTLE FUN ON HALLOWE'EN? THEN TRY MAKING THIS SCARY PICTURE USING MAGNETS! FIRST YOU'LL NEED A CLEAR PLASTIC WALLET, IRON FILINGS (FROM YOUR CHEMIST) A BAR MAGNET AND A LENGTH OF STICKY TAPE.

FIRST I TAPED THE MAGNET TO THE BACK OF THE CARD AND SLIPPED IT INTO THE WALLET. THEN I SPRINKLED IRON FILINGS OVER THE TOP OF THE CARD AND SEALED THE WALLET WITH STICKY TAPE DOWN EACH SIDE...

LASTLY WE TAPPED THE CARD LIGHTLY AND WATCHED THE IRON FILINGS FORM A PATTERN. THE FILINGS FOLLOWED THE INVISIBLE MAGNETIC FORCES ROUND THE MAGNET AND MADE THEM VISIBLE.

HERE'S ONE I MADE EARLIER! WE SHOWED IT TO BONNIE THE STUDIO DOG AND SHE WAS SO SCARED SHE BIT THE CAMERAMAN! WE DIDN'T HALF HAVE A GOOD LAUGH ABOUT THAT! WHY NOT MAKE ONE AND TAKE IT OUT TRICK OR TREATING, EH?

Frank Plank shuddered when he saw the policeman's gruesome iron-filings picture. "I think you're looking for a pirate, not a burglar, if you ask me. And I should know. I'm a detective!"

"I've always wanted to be one of those myself," PC Constable admitted.

"How very nice," Plank muttered and tried to close the door. PC Constable's size twelve boot was in the way. "If you'll excuse me, officer, I'm very busy just now," Plank said and pushed at the door.

But the constable had his orders. "Keep him talking," Auntie Gladys had said.

"Of course I have to be sure that you're not the burglar chap yourself," the policeman said.

"I certainly am not. My name is Frank Plank."

"And can you prove that, sir?"

"Of course I can!" He stepped outside and pointed to the brass plate with his name on. "You see. My name."

"Ah, but how do I know that you really are the Frank Plank whose name is on this sign? Have you some form of identification?"

"Yes... but it's in my jacket."

"Where's your jacket?"

"In the office."

"Ah! Hah-hah-hah!" the policeman laughed. "Once knew a chap who left his jacket in his office on a night like this. His front door keys were in his jacket. He stepped out of the front door and it slammed shut... just like this!" And PC Constable grabbed the door and quickly tugged it shut. "Would you believe it? He'd locked himself out of his office. Just goes to show – you should never leave your keys in the office when you go to answer the door."

"My keys are in the office," Frank Plank said blankly.

"Oh, dearie, dearie me!" the young policeman exclaimed. "You've gone and locked your silly old self out. Very careless of you. Just like the chap I was telling you about."

I gave a silent cheer and raced back to spread the important news. "Frank Plank's locked out. Go and get her, Auntie Gladys!"

Mr Wiggot lifted me upwards until I reached the window sill. Then I heard the rumble of a caterpillar tractor. Auntie Gladys appeared, driving a huge crane from the scrapyard. Dangling from the end was a thick metal disc. She brought it to the window, flicked a switch and turned the disc into a powerful electromagnet.

Suddenly every paper clip in the room flew to the window and hit it like hailstones.

Sally looked up from her chair. The chair began to move slowly towards the window. Sally watched, amazed, as my hand reached through the narrow window-opening, and my scissors sliced through the tape that held her hands. "Who are you?" she asked, after ripping the tape from her mouth.

"Your cousin Sam Spark, come to rescue you. Here, take the scissors, cut your feet free, then open the window further."

Moments later, Mr Wiggot had lowered me and gone back to help Sally to the ground. She gave Boozle a quick hug while he tried to lick the skin off her face.

At the corner of Dockyard Street the young policeman was standing. "Where's Frank Plank now?" the old caretaker asked.

"Ah, poor Mister Plank," he smiled. "I locked him out, just as we planned. He broke a window in the front door and let himself back in. That's when I arrested him... for breaking and entering. The squad car's just taken him away."

"Thank you, constable..." Auntie Gladys said, and looked at him closely. "I'm sorry, I don't know your name?"

"Constable."

"Yes, but what's your name?"

"Constable! My name's Constable Constable."

Auntie gave a weak smile. "Never mind. If you keep it up you'll soon be Sergeant Constable. Much more sensible. Goodnight!"

"Evening all," the policeman saluted. He called up to Mr Wiggot, "Oh, sir!"

Mr Wiggot turned and looked down. "Yes?"

"Sir, if you ever fancy joining the police force they'd be pleased to have you. I'm sure you'd pass the height test."

The two men walked off down the road and the street lights flickered on. A car pulled up at the kerb and we could hear the radio news...

AND HERE IS THE EIGHT O'CLOCK NEWS, BUT WE ARE UNABLE TO TELL YOU THE TIME BECAUSE THE ELECTRIC CLOCK STOPPED. BUT THE NEWS FROM DUCKPOOL IS THAT ELECTRIC POWER IS BACK. IT WASN'T AN ALIEN INVASION BUT SOMEONE AT THE ELECTRICITY BOARD WHO PUSHED THE WRONG BUTTON. AND REPORTS ARE COMING IN THAT A DEFECTIVE DETECTIVE HAS BEEN ARRESTED FOR THE KIDNAPPING OF SALLY SPARK. SHE IS BACK SAFE IN THE HANDS OF HER FAMILY, WHO PLAN TO ADOPT HER AND HER LOVEABLE DOG...

The radio snapped off and a voice from the car said, "But not for long!"

Sally gasped. I turned to the car. A sharp-faced, pointy-chinned woman with black hair stuck out a claw to grab Sally. "Cruella de Crunch!" she cried.

"Get in!" the woman ordered. "If I have to get out of my car then you'll be sorry!"

Sally stared in horror and looked at me for help. Suddenly there was a rumble and a clank and the electro-magnetic crane appeared. The magnetic disc swung down and fastened onto the roof with a clunk. It rose quickly into the air and swung the car over the scrap-yard wall.

"Well done, Auntie Gladys!" I cried.

She waved down. "This is what this machine is meant for. It picks up cars and drops them into this crusher. The car ends up in a cube of mangled metal just one metre across."

"You wouldn't do that to me!" Cruella de Crunch wailed through her window.

Auntie Gladys replied, "You'd do it to me if you were in the crane and I were in the car, wouldn't you?"

"Of course!" the woman with a face like a wood-axe answered.

"Fine!" Auntie Gladys said. She flipped a switch, to turn off the electricity and the magnet lost its power. The car dropped.

"Ooooh! Painful!" Sally sighed.

"She deserved it," Auntie Gladys said, as she climbed down and led me back home with my new sister.

"So what did Cruella de Crunch say?" Sally asked our auntie.

"Only one thing she could say!" our awesome auntie cackled... "Crunch!!!"

**Here is a list of experiments in this book.
Have you tried them all?**

* Science Notes*

✳ Science Notes✳

✳ Science Notes ✳

✴ Science Notes ✴

✳ Science Notes ✳